Miss Mousie's Blind Date

By TIM BEISER

Illustrated by RACHEL BERMAN

TUNDRA BOOKS

Published in Canada by Tundra Books, a Division of Random House of Canada Limited,
One Toronto Street, Suite 300, Toronto, Ontario M5C 2V6

Published in the United States by Tundra Books of Northern New York,
P.O. Box 1030, Plattsburgh, New York 12901

Library of Congress Control Number: 2011938763

Library and Archives Canada Cataloguing in Publication

Beiser, Tim, 1959-
Miss Mousie's blind date / by Tim Beiser ; illustrated by
Rachel Berman.

For ages 3-6.
ISBN 978-1-77049-251-6

1. Mice – Juvenile fiction. I. Berman, Rachel, 1947-
II. Title.

PS8603.E42846M58 2012   jC813'.6   C2011-906496-0

We acknowledge the financial support of the Government of Canada through
the Canada Book Fund and that of the Government of Ontario through the
Ontario Media Development Corporation's Ontario Book Initiative.
We further acknowledge the support of the Canada Council for
the Arts and the Ontario Arts Council for our publishing program.

ONTARIO ARTS COUNCIL
CONSEIL DES ARTS DE L'ONTARIO

Medium: watercolor and gouache on rag
Design: Erin Cooper
Printed and bound in China

1 2 3 4 5 6   17 16 15 14 13 12

For Morley, Daniel, and Rowan

— J.T.B.

For Maurice Sendak

— R.B.

Spring is such a funny thing –
    it wakes up all the plants
And makes our furry woodland friends
    go cuckoo for romance.
And so it was, one day in May,
    when stopping by the deli,
Miss Mousie's eye fell on a guy
    who turned her knees to jelly.

Matt LaBatt, the water rat,
  was such a handsome fellow!
His fur was black. His eyes were red.
  His teeth were lemon yellow.

He caught her eye and nodded "hi."
  She couldn't speak or squeak.
Miss Mousie's paws began to shake.
  Her little legs went weak.

The droll mole deli-owner gave the rat a Swiss on rye.
And viewing Matthew chewing it, Miss Mousie thought she'd die.
To catch the rat's attention, Mousie headed for the door
And coyly dropped a hankie from her pocket on the floor.

Matt shook his head. "Hey, Mole," he said,
  "Come fill my coffee cup.
And tell that fat girl by the door
  to pick her hankie up."

Miss Mousie twitched her nose and froze.
Can I believe my ears?
That awful rat has called me fat!
Her eyes filled up with tears.

She scampered to her burrow, and she hid there for a day,
Ashamed to go outside and hear what other folks might say.
Her chubby, tubby body would just be a cause for laughter.
She might as well decide to hide inside forever after.

One morning, without warning, at her door came several knocks,
And she found this invitation stuffed inside her letterbox:

"We've never met (at least not yet),
but, dear, tonight at eight,
Would you agree to dine with me?
I'll be your mystery date."

My goodness me! Who could it be?
And why this sense of mystery?
Is he aware that I am fat,
and, worse, my recent history?

She squeaked, "Oh, no! I dare not go!"
then raced to find a mirror.
"One look at me, and he will flee.
That much cannot be clearer."

"But in disguise? That might be wise!
    In fact, I think it's best."
So to her storage hole she stole
    and searched her wooden chest.
She found some bells and scallop shells,
    three tea towels made of cotton,
A tablecloth, wings off a moth,
    and pearls she had forgotten.

She took these things, and, with some strings,
    she made a gown so clever
That just to guess who wore that dress
    would take some folks forever.
And for her head, she found some thread
    and curtains made of lace,
Then made a crown of snails and veils
    to cover up her face.

Miss Mousie headed down the road
    inside that clever gown.
From looks she got, folks must have thought
    the circus was in town.

She was the cause of wild applause,
    loud shouts and cheers and whistles...

Which lasted till she took a spill
and landed in some thistles.

The thistle thicket was so thick
    and tangled with sharp brambles
That every thorn snagged what she'd worn
    and left her dress in shambles.

        Dead leaves upon her sleeves were stuck,
           and much to her dismay,
        As rain came down and soaked her gown,
           her big hat blew away.

At 8:08, she reached the gate at Mystery Date's address.
Her first blind date – and she was late!
And looking like a mess!

She sadly trudged up to the door and gave a fearful knock.
To her surprise what met her eyes was something of a shock.

Standing right before her was the mole who owned the deli!
She recognized him by his eyes and by his tubby belly –

But he had whiskers like a rat!
And hair black as a crow!
With squint and grin, he showed her in
and stepped upon her toe.

With an air quite debonair,
    the mole first tried to seat her
In funny spots, like flowerpots
    and on a carpet beater.

All through his hole,
the squinting mole could hardly find his way.
As Mousie gawked, the poor guy walked
smack into the buffet.

With such a crash,
his rat mustache was knocked in disarray.
And placed upon his face with paste,
it quickly dropped away.

Finally, he quite blindly sat her down upon a bench.
« *Café au lait, oui-oui soufflé?* »
he cooed in nonsense French.

Then to a chair with no one there,
he said, "This might be daring,
But I confess I love your dress
and that sweet hat you're wearing."

This nutty situation struck Miss Mousie as so funny
That she slapped her thighs and giggled
till her little eyes were runny.

"You're phony as boloney!"
Mousie laughed. "I call a truce.
No girl objects to men in specs.
Please wear yours, silly goose!"

"I played the same lame costume game.
Let's have another try:
I'm plain and fat – and that is that!"
The mole squeaked, "So am I!"

He set his jaw, then took her paw and said on bended knee,
"If you'll be you, then I'll be me."

Miss Mousie said, « *Oui-oui.* »

The End.